8'04   3.99

Book Two of

THE KLONDIKE KID

Trilogy

The Long Trail

D1304941

By Deborah Hopkinson

Illustrated by Bill Farnsworth

ALADDIN PAPERBACKS
NEW YORK LONDON TORONTO SYDNEY

BALDWIN PUBLIC LIBRARY

In loving memory of my father, Russell W. Hopkinson (1922–2003), who journeyed this long trail with courage and a twinkle in his eye

If you purchased this book without a cover, you should be aware that this book is stolen property. It was reported as "unsold and destroyed" to the publisher, and neither the author nor the publisher has received any payment for this "stripped book."

This book is a work of fiction. Any references to historical events, real people, or real locales are used fictitiously. Other names, characters, places, and incidents are the product of the author's imagination, and any resemblance to actual events or locales or persons, living or dead, is entirely coincidental.

First Aladdin Paperbacks edition July 2004

Text copyright © 2004 by Deborah Hopkinson
Illustrations copyright © 2004 by Bill Farnsworth

ALADDIN PAPERBACKS
An imprint of Simon & Schuster
Children's Publishing Division
1230 Avenue of the Americas
New York, NY 10020

All rights reserved, including the right of reproduction in whole or in part in any form.

Also available in an Aladdin library edition
Designed by Sammy Yuen Jr.
The text of this book was set in Palatino.

Printed in the United States of America
2 4 6 8 10 9 7 5 3 1

Library of Congress Control Number 2004102945

ISBN 0-689-86033-1

511 8517

~ TABLE OF CONTENTS ~

Ho, for the Klondike,
Ho, for the Klondike,
Ho, for the Klondike, ho!

Put on your pack
And don't come back
Till you fill your sack
On the northwest track.
Ho, ho, for the Klondike, ho!

CHAPTER ONE

~ **Stowaway** ~

I opened my eyes, and at first I couldn't remember where I was.

Then muffled shouts reached my ears.

"Good luck!"

"Bring back a sack of gold!"

A sharp, familiar whistle pierced the early morning air. I heard my friend Tag yell, "Hurray for the Klondike Kid!"

It all came back. I was a stowaway, sailing for gold.

• • •

As the steamer *Al-ki* made its way out of the Seattle harbor the shouts from the dock grew fainter. But it was noisy on the boat. Dogs barked endlessly. People clomped up and down in their heavy boots, talking and laughing. Every so often a horse neighed.

I stretched out my legs as much as I could, hoping my hiding place was a good one. Tag had helped me sneak aboard at midnight. While he distracted the watchman, I'd scurried down to the steamer's lower deck.

That's where I was now—in a large wooden chest, under a pile of rain slickers, boots, and coils of thick, salty rope. There were enough small cracks so I could breathe but not be seen.

My stomach growled. Reaching inside my pack, I pulled out one of Cook's biscuits. Right about now Cook would be waking up to fix breakfast for the gentlemen in the rooming house.

If I closed my eyes, I could imagine her bending down to pick up the sketch I'd slipped under her bedroom door last night. I'd done it one rainy morning while she was kneading bread. On the bottom I'd scribbled, "Mabel Cole, best cook in Seattle, drawn by David Hill, age 11, 1897."

It was the only good-bye present I had to give her.

It wouldn't take Cook long to guess where I was headed. But I knew she wouldn't give my secret away to Mrs. Tinker, the thin, tough woman who owned the rooming house. I tried to imagine what Cook would tell her.

"Davey has run off," Cook might announce as she poured Mrs. Tinker's coffee. "Mistress, you were kindness itself, letting that boy stay here after his mother died last winter. But it looks like he's hopped a train to New York, back to his momma's folks."

Well, in a way I *was* running off to my momma's folks. I was searching for my uncle Walt Thomas, Momma's only brother. But I wasn't heading to New York.

Like thousands of others, I was heading north—to the Klondike.

Thump! Thump!

Someone began kicking the wooden chest so hard I almost choked on my biscuit. I froze, trying not to make a sound.

"Rusty! Russell Clark, you stop that," came a girl's voice.

"Aw, be a nice sister and help me open it, Hannah," the boy replied. "Maybe there's gold inside."

Crack! Another hard kick. This one close to my head.

"There's no gold yet, silly. That comes later. Remember, this boat's taking us to Skagway, Alaska," the girl told him. "Dawson City and the Klondike River are still hundreds of miles from there, in Canada."

"I don't care. I *still* want to open it," Rusty persisted. "Come on, help me. The lid's heavy."

"All right. But promise you won't ever climb inside. Ma doesn't need for you to go missing," his sister warned. "It's hard enough for her to be making the trip alone with us and baby Ellen."

I heard huffs and puffs. Then light broke over my head. The chest opened.

"Nothing here but a bunch of rope and old gear," the girl said.

"Wait, I think I see a boot," her brother replied. "Maybe it'll fit me."

Above me ropes and rain slickers were pushed aside. In another second small fingers brushed my ankle.

"I touched something," the boy screeched. "A dead body!"

"Move and let me look," his sister

ordered, plunging her hands into the chest and throwing the gear aside.

Next thing I knew, I was staring into a pair of wide brown eyes. I shot her a warning look.

The girl stared for a second. Then, without a word, she piled the gear back over me. *Crack!* The lid crashed shut.

"You touched some old rain slickers, that's all," I heard her say. "Let's go back to Ma."

Even after their footsteps had trailed away, I could feel my heart pounding. *What now?* I wondered.

I knew I couldn't stay hidden in one spot for a whole week. But I'd hoped to keep out of sight until we were as far from Seattle as possible.

I had to be careful. It wasn't just the captain who might want to put me off the boat along the way. Two other men on board could ruin my plans of getting to Skagway.

Now I had this girl to worry about too. What if she told her mother? With my luck her mother might haul me up in front of the captain and make him leave me at Port Townsend, our first stop.

I'd better slip out now and find a new hiding place before she comes back, I decided.

At that moment a stern voice ordered, "I know you're in there. Come out!"

CHAPTER TWO

~ The Inside Passage ~

"Come out now," the voice repeated.

Slowly I pushed the gear aside and stuck my head up. My mouth dropped open when I saw those same twinkling brown eyes. This girl had tricked me!

"Fooled you, didn't I?" she chortled. "I tried to make my voice deep and low, like the captain's. But don't worry, I won't give you away. My name's Hannah Clark. What's yours?"

I wanted to shout at her to go away. At that moment a sailor came around the corner and waggled a long finger at me. "Hey, kid, what are you doin' in there?"

"Sorry, sir. We were just playing," Hannah said quickly. She grabbed my wrist. "Found you! Now it's my turn to hide."

Flashing a smile at the sailor, she pulled hard. I didn't have a choice. I scrambled out and stumbled after her.

"Well, now I know your name and that you're looking for your uncle," said Hannah a while later. We were huddled behind some crates and bales of hay piled on the deck. "But tell me: Who are you hiding from?"

"What . . . what makes you think I'm hiding from someone?" I sputtered.

"You keep looking over your shoulder," Hannah replied at once. Her sharp brown eyes studied me thoughtfully. "You can't really be worried about the sailors. They're all so busy, I bet they wouldn't even notice an extra kid. So, just who *are* you afraid of?"

A steady drizzle had begun. I didn't

mind, though. After hours down below, the cool, salty air felt good.

"I *do* know two men on this boat," I admitted. "One's a young photographer named Erik Larsen. Back in Seattle I asked him to take me to the Klondike as his helper. He said no, but I hope he'll change his mind once I turn up in Skagway. If he sees me before then, though, he might try to send me back."

"What about the other man?" Hannah asked, throwing her shawl over her head to keep off the rain.

"His name is Big Al—"

"Big Al!" Hannah cried. "Oh, I bet I know which one *he* is. How do you know him?"

"He and Erik both stayed at Mrs. Tinker's boardinghouse, where I lived. Big Al stole my money from the shed where I'd hidden it." I frowned, staring out at the gray water. "I had almost enough saved to buy my passage."

Big Al was a large, gruff man. He scared

me. "Maybe Big Al wouldn't do anything if he saw me," I went on, "but maybe . . ."

"Maybe he'd threaten to turn you in to the captain unless you went to work for him." Hannah raised her shoulders and growled, "Kid, I'm gonna make you pull my sled like a dog."

"This isn't a game, Hannah," I said sharply. "Some of these prospectors are rough fellows. All they care about is finding gold."

"I'm sorry, Davey," Hannah said at once, putting her hand on my arm. "Ma is always telling me to be more serious. I think you're doing a brave thing. You can count on me to help."

Hannah kept her promise. As the *Al-ki* steamed north along the Inside Passage, she brought me food two or three times a day.

I left my hiding place when I had to, mostly at night or when the passengers were at meals. Hannah and I discovered it wasn't hard to stay out of sight on deck. We found lots of places to hide among the piles of supplies and bales of hay.

Hannah also kept an eye out for Big Al. That was easy. Mostly he stayed below near the horse stalls, playing cards and talking with other men.

And after I pointed Erik Larsen out to her, Hannah didn't have much trouble keeping track of him, either. Erik spent most of the time in his berth or near the railing, seasick.

"He must have a weak stomach, because the seas aren't that rough. The islands to the west protect us from the open Pacific," I said to Hannah one afternoon. "I guess that's why they call it the Inside Passage."

"I haven't been seasick, but I sure am getting sick of the food on this boat," Hannah said, wrinkling her nose in disgust. "Nothing but oatmeal, stew, and beans. And from the letters Pa writes, it won't be much better in Skagway."

Hannah had told me about her family. Her father had gone to Skagway and built a cabin. He'd brought horses with him. Now he was working as a packer on the White Pass Trail, hauling supplies over the mountains for stampeders who had money to hire him and his horses.

"Pa told us the sure money is in having a business, not in looking for gold," she told me. "He says we can make a life there, as long as the gold rush is on."

"I wonder if my uncle Walt has found gold yet. His last letter was from up north, telling us he wanted to seek his fortune," I said thoughtfully. "That's why I have a feeling he's up there somewhere, looking for gold on the Klondike River."

"I hope you're right, Davey," said Hannah softly.

● ● ●

Late on the third day the steamer made a stop at Fort Wrangell. I was hiding in the chest when Hannah came close and whispered that the *Al-ki* would dock overnight on the island.

"Sounds like most folks plan to go ashore," she told me. "We are! Ma wants to try to find a restaurant for dinner. I'll bring you back some bread and butter if I can."

After Hannah left, I heard other passengers preparing to leave too. One man told his friend, "Let's go, Will. There's a brewery here with beer for two bits a quart!"

Before long the boat was strangely quiet. *Now is my chance to look around,* I decided. I wanted to find out if Dandy was on board.

Dandy had belonged to our neighbor, a lady we called Mrs. Mac. Dandy was more like a big dog than a horse. He liked to eat Mrs. Mac's daisies. Sometimes he even managed to barge into her kitchen and gobble up her apple pies.

When word reached Seattle that gold had

been discovered in the Klondike, men scoured the streets, buying up every horse and dog in sight. My landlady, Mrs. Tinker, didn't waste a minute before she sold her husband's loyal dog, Joe.

And when a horse trader offered Mrs. Mac money for Dandy, she took it. Later, once she heard how hard life would be for packhorses, Mrs. Mac changed her mind. By then Dandy was nowhere to be found.

I didn't have much hope that Dandy was on the *Al-ki*. Even if he was, I probably couldn't do anything to help my old friend. Still, I just had to look for him.

I made my way to where the horses were wedged in, side by side, in two long rows. Most looked worn out, their heads low and their sides heaving. I studied each one. No Dandy.

Face it, I told myself, *Dandy and Joe are gone forever, just like Momma.*

16

A black mare whinnied as I passed.

"You're scared and alone on this long journey too, aren't you, girl?" I said softly, stopping to pat her soft, velvety nose. "I wish I had an apple to give you."

At that moment I heard a shout, then quick footsteps behind me. Before I had time to move, a large, heavy hand grabbed my shoulder.

CHAPTER THREE

~ Discovered! ~

"Hey, kid. Leave them horses alone," a man boomed.

I froze. I recognized that voice: Big Al.

Big Al spun me to face him. He loomed over me, a huge bear of a man. Peering into my face, he frowned.

"Wait a minute, I know you. You're the kid from the rooming house," he cried. "The one who called me a thief. What's your name?"

I took a deep breath and tried to shrug his hand off. "Davey. Davey Hill. Now let me alone."

"Let you alone, eh? So you can go freeze your feet off in the Klondike, like the rest of these fools?" Big Al shook me a little. "Just about all you got is the clothes on your back, am I right?"

"My uncle's in the Klondike, waiting for me," I declared boldly, hoping it was true.

"Is that so?" Big Al let go of my shoulder and shook one thick finger in my face. "You called me a thief, but it seems to me you're a liar—and a stowaway to boot. If the captain has a lick of sense, he'll put you off here and pick you up on the way back to Seattle."

He reached out to grab me again, but I was quicker. Ducking, I slipped past him and began to run.

"I won't go back," I yelled over my shoulder.

I heard the heavy clomp of Big Al's boots behind me. I tried to think quickly. *Where could I hide now?*

I glanced back over my shoulder. I turned

a corner, then *crash!* I slammed into someone so hard I almost fell down.

"Davey!"

"Erik!" I gasped. Just my luck. The two men I'd tried most to avoid had both stayed on board.

Big Al appeared, puffing a little. He spoke first. "Is this your doing, Larsen, bringing this boy up here?"

Erik looked thinner than ever next to the big man. "I didn't know he was here, I swear. Davey asked to come along, but I said no."

Big Al glared. "I've been in the Klondike for the past year. I just returned to Seattle to buy some horses. I know what it's like up north. It's no place for a kid, I tell you. So, what do we do with him?"

I made a move to run, but Erik grabbed my arm. I shook it off and stood my ground. "I can't go back to Mrs. Tinker. Please let me be your helper, Erik."

Erik's bright blue eyes strayed to Big Al's

face. He sighed. "I suppose I can take him on."

"You don't know what you're doin', Larsen," Big Al spit, shaking his shaggy head. "You might get by in Skagway. But what about getting to the Klondike? Are you prepared to take this boy over that long trail?"

"I'm looking to make money taking pictures in Skagway and Dyea," Erik told him. "I might not even go to the Klondike."

Big Al leaned closer. "Maybe not," he growled. "But can you stop this kid?"

"It wasn't easy, but I've struck a deal with the captain," said Erik the next morning. "I'll pay for your passage with photographs."

"Thank you, Erik. I . . . I'm sorry about the way I acted in Seattle just before you left," I told him. "I had to pretend to be angry. I didn't want you to suspect I'd already made up my mind to come along no matter what."

"From now on I expect the truth from

you, Davey. Plus a lot of hard work," Erik said. His blue eyes looked worried. "Big Al is right about one thing: This country is rough. And we both have a lot to learn."

Now that Erik was paying for my passage, I was free to walk around the *Al-ki* right out in the open. Hannah and I spent hours on deck, listening to the cries of gulls and watching for whales and porpoises. It was the best place to be, for by now the whole boat smelled like a barnyard!

In the evenings the passengers gathered to tell stories or sing. Once, as we watched an enormous moon rise over the dark, glacier-topped peaks onshore, I even heard Big Al's deep voice join in.

Three days later we crowded on deck to get our first sight of Skagway. A sailor pointed toward shore. "See, there! The town's nestled in that valley between those hills."

"Klondike, here I come," chortled one

man. "I ain't leaving till I've struck gold."

"What are those clumps of white things?" Hannah wanted to know.

From the back of the group Big Al's voice called out, "Tents, miss. Skagway's nothing but a mess of mud and tents."

"How do we get ashore, Ma?" Rusty asked. "I don't see a dock."

"They haven't built one yet. Our luggage and supplies will be loaded onto a scow, a large, flat boat," explained Mrs. Clark, shifting baby Ellen from one hip to the other. "But we'll ride in a rowboat."

"Davey and I would be happy to assist you, Mrs. Clark," Erik offered.

Hannah poked me in the ribs. "Erik's nice," she whispered. "You'll see, everything will turn out fine."

As soon as the *Al-ki* anchored offshore, the boat exploded with activity. Miners scurried to locate their gear, animals, and feed. People shouted, running this way and that. It was easy to see how the gold rush had gotten its nickname: "the Klondike stampede."

Most stampeders had outfits weighing more than a thousand pounds, and sometimes two. Each outfit contained a year's worth of supplies—axes, hammers, rope, picks, and shovels. For food there were sacks full of cornmeal, flour, sugar, beans, dried fruit, coffee, and tea. Many stampeders had brought bales of hay for their horses, or cornmeal and bacon to feed their dogs.

Erik didn't have a large outfit yet. He hoped to earn money in Skagway taking pictures. Then, if he decided to go on to Dawson City, he'd buy more supplies. Still, even Erik had a lot of luggage to worry about. He'd brought a tent, cooking utensils, and some food, as well as several crates full of photographic equipment.

Before long the *Al-ki* was surrounded by rowboats. The rowers called out, "Ride to shore for twenty-five cents!"

Erik and I piled into one boat with Hannah's family, but all too soon it hit bottom. "We're still far from shore, but I'm afraid we'll have to walk the rest of the way across the tidal flats," said Erik.

Erik carried the baby and kept hold of Mrs. Clark's arm. Hannah held her mother's other hand. I helped Rusty, who kept falling down. Finally I picked him up and carried him.

"It's awful, like wading through mud!" Hannah cried, wrinkling her nose in disgust.

I nodded grimly. The muddy flats seemed endless. I kept staggering under Rusty's weight. "You're heavy for a little kid, Rusty," I gasped.

Suddenly Rusty let out a yell. "There he is! It's Pa. Pa, we're here!"

A tall, sturdy man made his way to us, arms outstretched. I was glad to hand Rusty over. He swept Hannah up in his arms too, then planted a kiss on his wife's cheek. They looked so happy together.

I swallowed hard, trying not to cry. I could hardly remember when I'd been part of a family.

But Hannah hadn't forgotten me. A minute later she ran over and grabbed my hand. "Well, good-bye, Davey. We're going home to our new cabin. Come see us soon."

"All right. And, um . . . thank you. Thanks for everything, Hannah," I sputtered, then turned to follow Erik.

"Take care of yourself, Davey," she called out after me. "I hope you find what you're looking for."

CHAPTER FOUR

~ Dogs, Men, Horses, ~ and Mud

"I've got a job," announced Erik the next evening outside the tent. We'd found an empty patch on the beach to camp, wedged in among hundreds of other tents, crates, and boxes.

"A job?" I asked, surprised.

"A photographer named Lars Heller has beaten me to it. He's already set up a studio here, and he's agreed to hire me as his assistant," Erik explained. "I'll deliver Heller's pictures to stampeders, but I'll have the chance to take my own photographs too."

"But, but . . . I thought you'd start your

own business," I protested. "I thought I'd be your helper."

"You still can, Davey. This just means we can use Heller's studio to develop photographs," Erik replied. His blue eyes sparkled with excitement. "There's lots to do. The more miners who buy pictures, the more work I'll have. Did you bring along that whistle you used in Seattle to sell newspapers?"

"I sure did. Wait, I'll try it out." I reached into my pocket and pulled out a small whistle. My friend Tag had given it to me the day the steamer *Portland* arrived, bringing the first word of gold in the Klondike.

I blew two short blasts on the whistle and called out, "Get your scenic pictures here!"

"That's wonderful." Erik chuckled. "We make a good team."

Erik and I *did* make a good team. And it wasn't long before I discovered that Erik really counted on me.

To begin with, Erik wasn't much of a cook. After a few days of eating his own meals of beans and oatmeal crusted with black, Erik threw up his arms and thrust the frying pan at me. "You give it a try, Davey. I burn everything!"

"I like to cook. I had a great teacher," I told him with a grin, remembering all the times I'd helped Cook in the rooming-house kitchen. "My biscuits are almost as light as Cook's were."

Erik wasn't good at other practical things either. He sometimes wandered for hours taking pictures of the grand scenery, forgetting all about the miners he was supposed to photograph.

And as for doing errands in Skagway, well, Erik left that up to me. "Davey, this is the most confusing place I've ever seen," he said. "Dogs, horses, and men everywhere. I keep tripping over piles of supplies. Why, I still can't find my way back to our tent without getting lost."

I laughed, but I had to agree: Skagway *was* confusing. The town was being built before our eyes. Nothing stayed the same from one day to the next. In the morning I'd walk by a rough, wooden frame building. The next afternoon I'd go the same way and realize the building was gone—moved to clear the way for a new street.

Every day more boats arrived, full of hopeful Klondike stampeders. They came from all over America, and even from other countries. There were mostly men, but some women, too. They'd left jobs and families, scraping together every last cent to follow their dreams of gold.

In Skagway the stampeders all worried about the same thing: how to get hundreds of pounds of supplies over the mountains. Some could afford to hire packers with horses, like Hannah's pa, or the strong, sturdy Tlingit Indians who worked as packers, carrying enormous loads on their backs.

But most would have to get over the mountains on their own. Then they'd spend the winter at Lake Lindeman or Lake Bennett, building boats to take them down the Yukon River to Dawson City.

I had my best luck selling photographs to newcomers, before the thought of the long trail ahead discouraged them. I'd blow my whistle and march up to a group of stampeders as they struggled to sort out their supplies or load their horses.

"This is your lucky day, folks," I'd say. "My associate, Erik Larsen, is a world-famous photographer. Mr. Larsen can take your picture, so you can send it home to your family. Don't you want them to see what you look like, covered with mud, before you strike it rich in the Klondike?"

People would laugh, and soon I'd arrange for them to pose for Erik. After Erik developed the photograph in Heller's studio, we'd put it in an envelope and deliver it.

I loved living in a tent and roaming the muddy paths of Skagway. Only one thing bothered me. No matter how hard I looked, I couldn't find anyone who knew my uncle. I asked everyone I met, "Have you ever seen a young fellow by the name of Walt Thomas?"

The answer was always the same. "No, kid. I ain't seen nothing but mud, sorry-lookin' horses, and men tuckered out from packing loads on the long trail."

Each morning I made oatmeal, bacon, and coffee on our stove. After breakfast, while I cleaned up, Erik headed out with his tripod, camera, and unexposed glass plates. Later he went to the studio to develop the pictures he'd taken.

At the end of the day we'd meet back at the tent. Sometimes, if it wasn't too rainy, I sat outside and sketched. Back in Seattle I'd spent hour after hour sketching boats in the harbor. Now I just wanted to draw animals, maybe because I felt so sorry for them up here.

Most of the miners had come from factories or offices. They'd never handled a packhorse before. Some didn't even know how to tie a knot. I saw horses with backs raw from wet and wrinkled blankets. Many had bad cuts on their legs. I looked for Dandy but never spotted him.

"That's a sad-looking horse you've drawn there," said Erik one evening. I had put my sketchbook down to begin cooking up some beans and bacon. "I hear more are dying every day on the Skagway trail over White Pass."

"That's the trail Hannah's pa works on, isn't it?" I asked, stirring the beans.

Erik nodded, pouring strong, black coffee into a tin cup. "I wanted to talk to you about Hannah's family, Davey."

I looked up, curious.

Erik was silent for a minute, sipping his

coffee. He seemed to be thinking hard about what to say next. "I saw Mrs. Clark yesterday. She's offered to let you stay in their cabin for the winter. I think it'll be for the best."

"I don't mind staying here with you, even when it gets cold," I protested. "I'm earning some money on my own doing errands. My wool blanket is fine for now, but soon I'll have enough to buy a canvas sleeping bag, too."

"I might not be here much longer, Davey."

"But . . . but . . . where are you going?"

"Heller's planning to leave for Dawson City with his brothers this winter," Erik said slowly. "He's going to set up a studio there. If I can get to Dawson on my own, he's offered me a job."

Erik stared into his coffee cup. "I've decided to go as soon as I buy an outfit," he said softly. "You'll be safe here with the Clarks."

I stopped stirring the beans. They'd probably burn, but I didn't care. I sputtered, "You mean . . . you're heading to the Klondike without me?"

"Davey, you came to look for your uncle, not for gold," Erik said. "If your uncle is in Dawson City or staking a claim on the Klondike River, he'll probably head back here sooner or later. It's too dangerous to take you over the pass."

"I've been pulling my own weight, Erik. I've sold lots of photographs," I pointed out. "And without me you wouldn't eat!"

I took a long breath. "I thought we were a team."

Then I threw down the spoon and stormed off.

CHAPTER FIVE

⁓ **The Long Trail** ⁓

"**D**avey!" Erik called after me, but I didn't stop.

I ran all the way to Broadway, Skagway's main street. Not that it was much of a street. It was mostly a muddy path lined by board-walks, large tents, and a few rough wooden shacks.

I had to push past men on every corner. In front of one saloon a few stampeders were arguing about which trail to take over the mountains.

"I'd rather use packhorses and try the Skagway trail over White Pass," I heard one

39

say. "The Chilkoot Pass on the Dyea trail is just too steep for horses."

"I tried White Pass and turned back," another man put in. "I'm heading to Dyea. The trail that starts there might take three months, packing load after load, but you *can* get over."

If I were strong enough, I'd march right up to them and hire myself out as a packer, I thought as I tramped past in the mud. But I was just a kid. And no one wanted a kid tagging along. Not even Erik, who was supposed to be my friend.

"Davey! Hey, wait up!" I turned to see Hannah striding toward me.

"Why haven't you come to visit?" she asked. "Ma had a long talk with Erik yesterday. I heard you're coming to stay with us this winter."

"No!" I cried sharply.

Then, seeing Hannah's face, my voice softened. "It's not that I don't like you or your folks. It's just that I want to go to the Klondike with Erik. I have to keep looking for Uncle Walt. No one here in Skagway has seen him. He just has to be in Dawson City."

"Probably Erik's just scared to take you along, Davey," Hannah said. "Pa says it's a long, hard trail even for a grown man."

"Nothing's going to happen to me," I protested. "I'm more worried about Erik going by himself."

"Well, try to talk to him again," advised Hannah. "Maybe he'll change his mind."

By the time I made my way back to the beach, hundreds of candles lit the tents. Erik was sitting on a crate, trying to scrape burned food off a frying pan. The coffeepot was overturned; dishes were scattered here and there. It looked like a runaway horse had plowed through camp.

"I got up to look at those clouds hanging over the mountains. I thought it would make a fine photograph," began Erik sheepishly. "When I smelled something burning, I ran

back so fast I tripped over everything."

Erik sighed. "I give in, Davey."

"You give in? Does that mean I can come along?"

Erik nodded. "You're right. We're a team. As they say, 'Klondike or bust!'"

When I fell asleep, I still had a grin on my face.

At first Erik wanted to buy horses and head over White Pass. But Hannah's pa warned us against it.

"Before long everyone will be calling it the Dead Horse Trail," Mr. Clark told us. "That trail is brutally hard. Every day more horses are being driven to death."

"Do you remember Big Al? Rusty and I saw him in town the other day," Hannah put in. "He's packing now on the Chilkoot Trail."

"But I thought he had horses," I said, remembering how Big Al had stayed near the horses on the *Al-ki*.

Hannah's pa nodded. "For a while he did. I guess he figured he could make more money packing on his own. Or maybe he couldn't stand to see the trail littered with dead horses."

Mr. Clark sighed. "I don't know how much longer I can stand it myself. A few more runs, then I'm thinking of starting a business here in town."

"It sounds as if the Chilkoot Pass is the way for us," said Erik. "Can it be done in winter?"

Hannah's pa rubbed his beard thoughtfully. "Yup. The native Tlingit Indians have been using this trail for years. But it won't be easy. By the time you get your outfit together, the trail will be covered with snow and the Dyea River will be frozen. You can pull your gear on sleds as far as Sheep Camp. But from there it's steep. You'll have to ferry your supplies on your back, one load at a time."

"How far is it?" I wanted to know.

"From Dyea it's about sixteen miles to the summit of Chilkoot Pass. After that it's ten miles to Lake Lindeman. Some folks stop there to build boats. But most go a few more miles to Lake Bennett, where the White Pass Trail ends," explained Mr. Clark. "A large tent city has grown up there. You can camp until May, when the ice is out of the Yukon River. By the time you've carried two or three loads a day, you'll have walked hundreds of miles."

"Hundreds of miles," Erik repeated slowly. "That *is* a long trail."

Hannah's pa looked at Erik closely. "You're a thin fellow. Are you sure you can handle packing day in and day out, and still watch out for this boy?"

Erik flushed. "This rough life is new to me. But I want to try, and so does Davey."

Hannah's pa sighed. His voice sounded tired. "I just hope you know what you're in for."

From then on Erik and I worked day and night to get ready. Supplies were more expensive than in Seattle. Mostly we bought from stampeders who'd already given up and decided to go back to their families. They'd never camped out in mud, rain, and cold before. And the thought of spending a harsh winter in a tent, before they even reached the Klondike, had been too much for them.

It took all fall to earn enough money. At last, in January, we'd gathered about fifteen hundred pounds of food and supplies. It seemed like a lot, but we knew the Canadian Northwest Mounted Police were stationed in a hut at the top of Chilkoot Pass. To prevent starvation, they'd made a rule that no one could enter Canada without enough provisions for a year. We'd have to pay a customs duty on all our supplies too.

Finally the day came. After a farewell dinner with Hannah and her family we loaded our outfit on a boat to make the short trip over to the town of Dyea, where the trail began. At least, it was supposed to be a short trip.

"The boat should take an hour," said Erik. "My stomach should be able to handle that."

Poor Erik. A bitter winter wind made the water rougher than usual. The boat rolled and pitched for nearly two hours. By the time we landed, both of us were sick, wet, and cold.

"Let's find someplace where we can thaw out," said Erik between chattering teeth.

We stumbled through the small town of Dyea. Like Skagway, it had a few hotels and eating houses. We spotted a small restaurant and headed toward it.

Suddenly I noticed a sign on a nearby tent that read DOG HOSPITAL.

"Got a dog that needs taking care of?" asked the man standing in front. "For ten dollars I'll keep any sick or hurt dog for a month and get it ready to work the trail again."

"I'm looking for a dog I knew in Seattle," I told the man. "An old black dog named Joe."

"Sorry, kid," said the dog man, shaking

his head. "I don't have one like that. A lot of them don't last long up here, you know."

Later, as Erik and I warmed ourselves before a woodstove in the restaurant, I thought about Dandy, Joe, and all the other horses and dogs who'd been brought north.

"I don't like the way folks are treating dogs and horses," I told Erik. "I wish there were a horse hospital. But I guess they just shoot them."

"Davey, I can't tell you to give up hope of finding your uncle," he said slowly. "But I think you should face the fact—you'll probably never see Dandy or Joe again."

Erik put his hand on my shoulder. "Since we're here, partner, how about a hot meal? We can get beans, bacon, dried peaches, and tea for seventy-five cents. We're going to need our strength for the long trail."

CHAPTER SIX

∾ **On Chilkoot Pass** ∾

Next morning Erik and I stood silently in front of our mountain of supplies. My heart sank. There was so much! How would we ever carry it all?

We had our bulky canvas tent, stove, canvas sleeping bags, wool blankets, an iron stove, a frying pan, and a coffeepot. There were large canvas sacks packed full of flour, beans, coffee, dried apples, oatmeal, and cornmeal. Erik didn't have the usual miner's pick and shovel, but his photography case weighed nearly fifty pounds. In it he'd packed his camera, lenses, glass plates, tripods, and other supplies.

"You did a good job of rounding up all the food, Davey," said Erik, pulling his hat down over his ears to keep them warm.

"We have so much, it'll probably take us until spring to carry it over Chilkoot Pass," I replied, pulling on my wool mittens.

Erik laughed and pulled out the rough map Hannah's pa had sketched for us. "Well then, we'd better get started. We'll haul our first load to Finnegan's Point, about six miles from here."

I looked at our two oak sleds. "I bet we can move everything that far in about four days."

"Let's load one sled with about two hundred and fifty pounds," Erik suggested. "I'll pull that. And we'll put another hundred pounds on your sled. Think you can haul that much?"

"I'm strong," I told him, stomping my feet on the snow to keep them warm. "Let's go."

• • •

"At least this first part of the trail is level," Erik called to me an hour later as we made our way along the frozen Dyea River. "Is your load too heavy?"

"No, I'm fine," I said. Yet by noon my shoulders and legs had begun to throb.

Even worse, I was hot and sweaty whenever I pulled the sled, but as soon as we stopped, I felt chilled. So no matter how much it hurt, I didn't stop much. I just kept telling myself that every step was bringing me closer to Uncle Walt.

Finnegan's Point was a cluster of tents, shacks, and cabins, including a restaurant, a blacksmith shop, and of course, a saloon.

"We can leave each load beside the trail until we've moved our whole outfit," Erik said, panting a little. "That's what everyone's been doing. So far folks up here have been honest."

After covering our boxes and crates with canvas, we ate some hardtack, then set off back down the trail, pulling the empty sleds behind us. By the time we got back to Dyea, where we'd pitched our tent the night before, I was so tired I could barely cook supper.

"So far, so good! We walked our first twelve miles today," Erik said brightly when we turned in. "Are you ready to pull another load tomorrow, Davey?"

I grunted sleepily, too exhausted to answer. Every muscle and bone ached.

Next thing I knew, it was morning again.

It took us four days to move our outfit to Finnegan's Point. The last trip, hauling our bulky tent, was the hardest. By then, I figured, we'd walked a total of forty-eight miles back and forth.

Our next camping stop was Canyon City, which wasn't a city at all, just a few log cabins. After we'd hauled all our goods there, we rested for a day, pitching our tent on the solid ice on the Dyea River. We cut spruce boughs to put under our sleeping bags.

When we awoke late the next morning, I cooked bacon, oatmeal, and huge stacks of pancakes. *Cook would be proud of me,* I thought.

We left Canyon City for Sheep Camp, four miles up the canyon. The trail headed uphill from here, rising steadily. At first I gasped for breath with each step. But as the days went by I got stronger. I could pull heavier loads. The return trip for the next load was easier now too, since we could ride our sleds down the trail.

Sheep Camp was a busy cluster of tents, shacks, yapping dogs, stray horses, and hundreds of stampeders. It was our last chance to chop firewood and gather kindling to use in our stove. After this we'd be above the trees, out in the open, harsh winds of Chilkoot Pass.

"It's too steep for sleds from here on,"

said Erik one morning as I set up our stove on the hard-packed snow. "We'll have to carry each load four miles to the Scales. From there we climb the last steep part, called the Golden Stairs, to the top of Chilkoot Pass."

"What's the Scales like?" I wanted to know.

"From what I hear, it's a wretched, windswept place. It got its name because there are scales there, where packers weigh their loads. Most packers charge more to carry goods up to the summit," Erik said. He paused, his blue eyes worried. "It's not going to be easy. Can you do it, Davey?"

I gritted my teeth. "I'm not turning back now."

This is it, I thought the next morning when I opened my eyes. *Today I get my first glimpse of Chilkoot Pass.*

Erik was still asleep, but I rolled out of my sleeping bag and got busy. As usual, the water in our buckets had frozen during the night. I fed kindling into the stove, thawed the water, and began to cook breakfast. Still no sign of Erik.

Poking my head into the tent, I called, "The oatmeal's lumpy and the coffee's hot, Erik."

Erik groaned. "Sorry, Davey. Seems like I ache all over. I was up with a sick stomach in the night. I think the water is bad. But I'll be ready soon."

"One, two, three . . . one, two, three." I counted each step, bent almost double with the weight on my back.

I got used to other men passing me by. Once, an entire Tlingit Indian family, including a mother and a girl my age, went by packing loads that looked much heavier than mine. I wondered if I could carry more weight if I used a head strap, as they did. I wondered, too, what they thought of their

old trail being invaded by thousands of strangers.

It wasn't even noon, but it seemed we had been climbing for hours. The day was so overcast and gray, it felt like late afternoon. My breath came in ragged gasps. *Five more steps before resting*, I told myself. *Now five more.*

Up ahead I spied a flat area. That must be the Scales, a cluster of tents and a few shacks, swarming with dogs and men. Just beyond, a thin black line cut into a steep white cliff. I stepped to the side of the trail and stared up.

And that's when I realized that the line was made up of men. Each one was plodding slowly, painfully, to the top of Chilkoot Pass.

I wanted to cry.

It had taken me hours to climb this far, with only thirty or forty pounds on my back. The rest of our outfit waited four miles back at Sheep Camp. It would take us weeks and weeks of trips, up and back, to carry it this far. And then we'd face the steepest, hardest climb of all.

I turned to see Erik coming up the trail. He was stooped low, planting a stick with each step. His face looked as pale and cold as the snow around us.

Suddenly he stepped off the trail and collapsed against a snowbank. He closed his eyes and groaned weakly.

Erik's too sick to go on, I realized. *It's impossible. We're not going to make it.*

We were stranded on Chilkoot Pass.

CHAPTER SEVEN

~ An Unexpected Rescue ~

"Erik, Erik! Open your eyes!" I cried, shaking him hard.

At last he sat up a little, holding his head in his hands. "Dizzy . . . ," he murmured. "I feel dizzy."

One by one other miners passed us. Most were bent down almost double under their loads. They didn't give us a second glance.

There's no one to help us, I realized. *What should I do?*

I tried to decide what would be best. I could leave Erik here and get help up ahead at the Scales. Or maybe I could try to hold

Erik up as we walked. If I could just get him to one of the eating houses up ahead, maybe a hot drink would revive him. But was I strong enough to support him?

No matter what, he couldn't stay here for long. It was getting colder every minute. I glanced at the gray sky. If it began to snow, he'd freeze.

"Erik, it's time to go," I said loudly, close to his ear. "There's a restaurant at the Scales. We can have some nice hot coffee. Try to stand up now."

Pulling hard, at last I got Erik to his feet. He wobbled uncertainly for a minute, then fell back onto the snow with a groan.

Suddenly a booming voice called out, "Well, ain't this a fine sight. What do we have here?"

Big Al, an enormous canvas bag strapped to his back, leaned against his walking stick and stared at us.

I glared back. Something about this man made me so angry I spoke without thinking.

"He's sick, not that you care. Just go on by and leave us alone. We don't want your help."

Big Al threw back his head and laughed so hard ice crystals sprayed off his beard. "You may not *want* my help, kid. But it sure looks like you need it. What happened?"

"Why should I tell you?" I cried. "You're just a bully and a thief. You stole my money."

Big Al threw down his stick and grabbed the front of my jacket in his fist. "Listen, kid. Your landlady in Seattle gave me that shed to sleep in. One day I walked in and found you messin' with my stuff, or so I thought. If you had money hidden in there, I ain't the one who took it."

I stared, my mouth open. "You . . . you're not?"

"No, I'm not. Why, I bet you never even had the guts to ask your landlady if she cleaned out the shed before she rented it out to me, did you?" Big Al asked, his face close to mine. "It was easier to blame it on me."

"I'm a sourdough, a man of the North," he went on. "I don't steal or lie. I'd rather carry a pack myself on this trail than watch another horse die on White Pass. I live by a code of honesty, and I expect my friends to do the same."

I hung my head. Big Al was right. He was so gruff and scary I *had* blamed him right away, even though I knew Mrs. Tinker was so greedy she'd even sell an old dog to make a few bucks.

I kicked at the snow with the toe of my boot. "I . . . I'm sorry."

Big Al let go of my coat and picked up his stick.

"So, Klondike Kid," he said, his brown eyes twinkling. "Are we friends?"

He stuck out his hand. I shook it.

"All right, then," said Big Al, rubbing his beard. "Now that we're square, let's get Larsen someplace warm before he freezes his hands off. We want him to be able to keep taking those pretty pictures, after all."

Big Al swung his own load off his back

and dug out a place for it in the snow alongside the trail. He strapped Erik's load onto his own back. Then he grabbed the young photographer by the arms. "Come on, then. Follow me."

Big Al was practically carrying Erik, but I still had to move fast to keep up. I glanced at the steep mountain ahead. Even this close the climbers looked no larger than ants, marching in single file to the top.

When we reached the Scales, Big Al barged into one of the small frame buildings half buried in deep snowdrifts. He beckoned to a young woman. "Hello there, Vernie. Got a young feller here who needs some help."

"Friends of yours, Al?" she asked, nodding toward Erik and me.

Big Al laughed under his breath. "Cheechakos from Seattle, like half these fools." Cheechakos, I knew, was what the Indians called newcomers.

Big Al turned to me. "You stayin' with him,

or are you strong enough to come along?"

"Come along where?" I asked stupidly.

"It's early afternoon yet. I still aim to take a load to the top of Chilkoot Pass. But if it's too much for you . . ." Big Al didn't finish his sentence. His dark eyes seemed to be laughing at me.

I hesitated, glancing back at Erik. At that moment Erik opened his eyes. He looked at Big Al and me and tried to smile. "I just need a little rest. I won't let you down, Davey, I promise. Go on with Al."

The young woman smiled at me. "Don't worry, Al won't bite. We'll watch your friend tonight, and he'll be set to go with you in the morning."

I took a deep breath and turned to face Big Al. "All right. I'm ready."

We made our way to the foot of the snowy cliff. Right away I could see why it was called the Golden Stairs. As far up as I could see, steps had been cut out of the ice. I wondered how many there were to the top. More than a thousand, I guessed.

"Once you step into line, keep up," Big Al told me. He pointed to the climbers snaking up the mountain, one step at a time. "If you gotta catch your breath, there's a snow bench to the side about every twenty steps or so. Some helpful packer has stuck posts along the trail and strung a guide rope between them, top to bottom, over the snow. If you need to, you can just reach down and grab the rope with one hand, holding your walking stick in the other. Got it?"

I nodded, gritting my teeth. "Yeah, I got it."

"See you on top, then. Try not to get too far behind. We still have to slide back down on a side trail, the Peterson Trail, and get back to Sheep Camp tonight," warned Big Al, stepping out in front of me.

Then he called over his shoulder, "Don't look down. And remember, it's not your legs that will get you to the top. It's your will. Sheer will."

It's steep, I thought as I slipped into the line of climbers, *steeper than I ever imagined.*

It really was like climbing stairs. Only these stairs were hard-packed snow and ice. *Step, breathe. Step, breathe,* I repeated to myself again and again.

I tried not to worry about Erik. Most of all, I tried not to think what would happen to me if he turned back.

Here and there along the trail men had stepped out of line to rest. The sat silently on benches made of snow, their faces gritty with dirt, their eyes bloodshot. Only the dream of gold kept them going.

A little more than halfway up I had to stop. My muscles burned with pain. My lungs hurt as I gulped in the cold air. There was nothing else to do. I stepped out of line and leaned against my stick, my knees shaking.

Big Al had warned me not to look down, but I did anyway. I felt so dizzy I was afraid I'd fall over. I stumbled over and fell onto the snow bench.

After a minute a man left the line and collapsed beside me. He managed to croak, "This your first trip up, kid?"

I nodded, too winded to speak. My head ached. My throat felt scratchy and dry. I wanted to be in that warm hut with Erik. Even more, I wanted to be in Cook's cozy kitchen, eating fluffy white biscuits and drinking hot tea.

"Well, this is my twentieth trip, and it don't get much easier." The man narrowed his eyes. "You look pretty beat, kid. Are you sure you can keep going?"

I tried to move, to show him. I strained against the pack, then fell back again.

It was no use. I couldn't get up.

CHAPTER EIGHT

~ Klondike or Bust! ~

"Hey you, kid! Hey, Klondike Kid!"
I twisted my head and looked up. Above me Big Al had stepped out of line too.

He waved, then cupped his hands together and hollered, "Get up! I ain't coming down."

Feebly I waved back. I remembered Big Al's words. "It's not your legs. . . . It's your will."

I have to get up, I told myself. *I have to show Big Al I have the heart to make it.*

Planting my stick in the snow, I leaned forward.

69

"Here, I'll give you a boost," offered the man beside me, pushing me up.

"Thanks," I told him, standing up at last. "Well, I'm off. Good luck."

A minute later I managed to slip back into line as another climber stepped out for a rest. It was so steep I hardly had to bend down to grab the guide rope. I took a deep breath, planted my walking stick, and pulled myself up the next step. And the next.

I wasn't giving up.

About an hour later I felt a strong hand grab mine and pull me over the edge. I collapsed into a deep snowdrift.

"Welcome to the top, kid," said Big Al, that same twinkle in his eyes. "I didn't think you could do it, but you surprised me. Not bad for your first trip."

Suddenly I laughed out loud.

"What are you laughing about?" Big Al

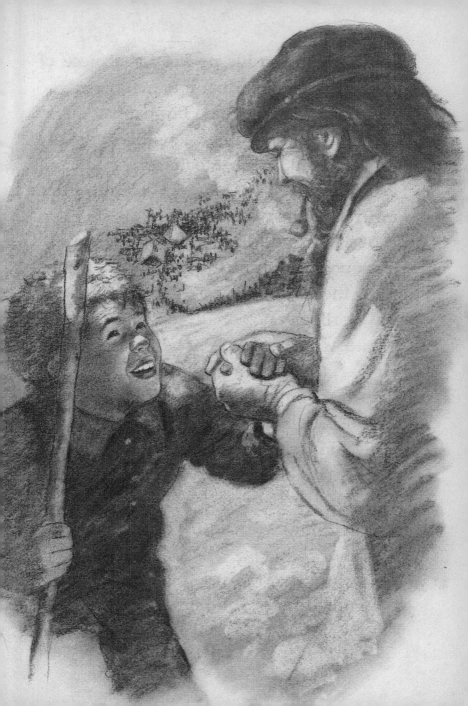

said, fumbling in his pocket for a piece of dried apple and handing it to me.

"I don't know. I guess I'm happy," I told him, still gasping a little. "I . . . I never really believed I could make it to the top of Chilkoot Pass. But I did. Now I know I can travel this long trail all the way to the Klondike."

And so would Erik, I felt sure of it now. We would carry our loads, one by one, to the top of the Golden Stairs, even if it took us until April.

And who knows? Maybe Big Al would help us. Then when spring came, we'd be ready to set out on the Yukon River, heading for the Klondike.

Big Al put his hand on my shoulder. This time his twinkling brown eyes looked kind. "You still believe your uncle's in the Klondike, don't you, kid?"

"Yes. Yes, I believe he is," I told Big Al, turning my face toward Canada. "And I'm not giving up till I find him."

AUTHOR'S NOTE

Although Davey Hill, Big Al, and Erik Larsen are fictional characters, their experiences in the Klondike are based on actual events. In July 1897 word reached Seattle that gold had been discovered on a tributary of the Klondike River in Canada. With the country in an economic depression, thousands jumped at the opportunity for adventure and the possibility of striking it rich. Seattle and other cities became jumping-off points, where eager stampeders bought their supplies.

The most popular route north was through the Inside Passage to Skagway, Alaska. From there, two grueling trails led over the mountains, to either Lake Lindeman or Lake Bennett, where stampeders built boats to take them down the Yukon River to the boomtown of Dawson City, near the Klondike River.

Many stampeders met with disappointment. Some gave up even before they made it over either Chilkoot Pass or White Pass. Most of those who made it to the Klondike found that the richest stakes had been claimed long ago.

Thanks to frontier photographers like E. A. Hegg and P. E. Larson, many unforgettable images of the Klondike stampede have survived. Looking at pictures of packhorses, sled dogs, and tired climbers on Chilkoot Pass, we can almost imagine ourselves there, hoisting packs onto our backs and starting up the Golden Stairs.

FURTHER INFORMATION AND READING

There are many wonderful unpublished and published accounts of the Klondike stampede. Three especially helpful books were *Faith of Fools: A Journal of the Klondike Gold Rush*, the journal of William Shape (1867–1960); journalist Edwin Tappan Adney's *The Klondike Stampede*; and Pierre Berton's *The*